D0604992

ARDIE'S BIG SECRET

Rosilyn Seay

To my family and extended family.
To all the teachers and educators who care enough to make a
difference in the life of a young person.

ISBN 978-0-9985576-4-9

Library of Congress Control Number: 2017947217

Printed and Bound in United States of America
PicBooks Publishing
http://picbookspub.com

Contents

Chapter One
Keeper of Secrets

I, Ardie Smith, am now the number one keeper of secrets.
I was the only one who knew about a special surprise for
my family. I promised to keep it a secret from them.
And nobody got it out of me; not my mom, my dad, or
my little brother, Jamie.
I only told my teacher, Miss Tucker, because she was not
in my family.

Keeping anything from my parents was not easy.

They knew me too well.

That's why I tried to stay away from them.

So, I kept finding things to do outside or in my room.

I did this for days and thought it was working.

Then one day, while I was practicing soccer, my dad came outside.

"What's up, Son?" he asked.

"Nothing, Dad. Just practicing," I answered.

"Buddy," he said, "with that goofy grin you've been wearing, I think there is more going on than that."

"Goofy grin, Dad?" I asked. I knew he'd just made that up.

"Yeah," he said. "That's what I call that smile right there. It's the one you always get when you're up to something."

"Uh, up to something? Like what?" I asked.

Dad just laughed. He was already at the door.

He turned and said, "Don't worry, Son. Sooner or later, I will find out what's really going on. I always do."

Then he went inside. No way was I going to follow him in. Sometimes, he almost seemed to have mind reading superpowers. If he did then I was safer outside.

As soon as Dad closed the door, I dropped the soccer ball.
I climbed up on the porch rail, spread my arms out, and
started tightrope walking.
I had wanted to try that forever.
I was almost halfway across the rail when I looked up.
My mom was there. She seemed upset.
"Ardwick Edward Smith," she said, "you get down from
there. Now!"

My mom waited for me to climb down.

Then she said, "I think it's time for you to go inside."

I was thinking that too. After all, nothing was working out the way I had hoped it would.

Instead of making it easier to keep my secret, I was only making Mom and Dad wonder why I was acting so weird.

Chapter Two
The Perfect Plan

The next day, after school, I told Miss Tucker everything.

"Ardwick," she said, "doing things to keep yourself busy was a good idea. But I have a suggestion."

"What?" I asked.

"Try doing a project," she answered. "Maybe you can center it around the surprise."

"What kind of project?" I asked.

"With your imagination," she said, "you'll think of something."

Grownups make hard stuff sound so easy.

But Miss Tucker had said that I would think of something.

So, I had to try. Plus, I liked the idea of my own secret project.

Luckily, it didn't take long. By bedtime I had a plan.

"Yes!" I said. "All I need are some tissues, a soccer ball, and stuff to put a banner together."

The next morning, I couldn't wait to start on my secret project.

First, I had to find paper, markers, tape, and string.

That's what I needed to make the banner.

There were colored markers on my bookshelf.

My old sneakers had two long strings.

But I couldn't find the paper or tape.

Getting them would be tricky. I had to go to my dad.

My dad never just gave you stuff. He always wanted to
know what it was for. So, I had to be careful.

"Dad," I said, "may I have some paper and tape? I need
them for a project."

"Sure, Buddy," he answered. Then he surprised me.

He didn't ask any questions. He just handed them to me.

"Thanks, Dad," I said, as I sped away.

Later, I remembered that I didn't have any tissues.
I went to get them from my mom.
With each step, I made myself sneeze, "AAA-CHOO!"
When I reached her, I sneezed loudly three times,
"AAA-CHOO! AAA-CHOO! AAA-CHOO!"
Using my sick voice, I asked, "Mom, may I have some tissues?"
She looked at me funny. But she gave me the tissues.

Chapter Three
The Wise and Wonderful Detective

"Mom didn't buy that at all," I thought, as I walked away.
"If I don't do something quick, she'll try to figure out
what I'm up to."

Then I smiled. I knew what to do.

Miss Tucker was right. It only took a little imagination.

The first step was to put a sign on my door that said,
"DETECTIVE AT WORK".

Next, I had to get my detective hat, badge, and dark glasses out of my treasure chest.

That's what I wore whenever I had a mystery to solve.

Some of the mysteries were from my detective books.

Others were family mysteries, like finding lost things.

If my family saw me wearing my detective stuff, they would leave me alone to solve my latest mystery.

That's why I went to the kitchen looking for Mom and Dad.
I had to make sure they saw me.
"Mom, when is dinner?" I asked.
"Soon," she answered. Then she added, "I see that 'Ardie the Wise and Wonderful Detective' is on the job."
I bowed, tipped my hat, and said, "At your service, madam."
Mom laughed. And, as I walked away, I couldn't stop smiling.

When I got back to my room, my little brother was there.
With Jamie around, I couldn't work on my banner.
I also couldn't leave my stuff where he might get to it.
So, I took it all outside. It would be safer in my red wagon.
On the way, I saw one of my soccer balls.
I dropped that in the wagon too.

Chapter Four

The Happy Dance

When Mom called me in for dinner, I covered the wagon and pushed it out of sight.

After dinner, Mom, Dad, and Jamie were all doing regular stuff.

I thought to myself, "I can't believe that I have such an important secret and nobody else knows about it."

I got so excited that I broke into a happy dance.

Of course, when I did that, everybody started staring at me. Still, it didn't matter because they thought that I was dancing to something from my music player.

That was ok with me. I just kept dancing.

Mom and Dad went back to doing what they were doing.
Before anyone could say anything, Jamie jumped up.
He grabbed at my music player and shouted, "Give me. I
want to dance too."

At first, I tried to grab it back. But I knew my parents.
Soon they would say something like, "Ardie, you should
share with your little brother."
So, I let go. I told Jamie, "You can listen for a while."
Then I left because I still had things to do.

19

Chapter Five
The Thing About Sharing

I walked away, but I kept looking back.

I was worried about Jamie having my music player.

After all, he was little. And no matter what you say or do, little kids find ways to break your stuff.

That was the one thing grownups did not seem to understand about sharing.

I kept walking and headed outside.
While everybody else was busy, this would be the
best time for me to finish my banner.
But first, I had to get the things from my wagon.
At least my secret project was the one thing I did not
have to share.

It's not that I didn't like sharing.

It's not even that Mom and Dad made me share all the time.

I just couldn't figure out the rules.

Ever since Jamie showed up, it seemed that everybody expected me to share all my stuff with him.

Only grownups knew why.

It didn't matter if it was my mother, my father, a teacher, a grandparent, or someone else.

They all said that they understood how I felt about my stuff.

But they still expected me to want to share it.

The grownups didn't even have to say a word.

They had this special stare.

They all knew how to use it.

And the stare was sometimes worse than words.

The only one who understood how I felt was my big brother, Jake.

After all, Jake had two little brothers, Jamie and me.

But, since Jake was far away, I could only talk with him on the phone.

That was how I got the news about the secret.
Jake called one day. He wanted to tell me
about a surprise he had planned.
He made me promise not to tell anyone,
especially not big mouthed Jamie.

25

Chapter Six
One Wet Cat

Now I was running out of time.
There were only a few days left until the surprise.
I had to hurry and finish my banner.

I spread everything out on the floor. It was easier that way.
Then I put one big letter on each sheet of paper.
I taped the sheets together into one long sign.
To make it easy to carry, I rolled it up and tied the string
around it. At last I had my banner!
Now I just had to wait for the big surprise.

A few days later, I got the phone call saying that it was time. I put the rolled-up banner, the ball, the tissues, and the tape back into my wagon.

As I pulled the wagon around front, my dad had been watching me. He stopped washing his car. He could tell that something was up.

My dad watched a little while longer.
Then he said, "Buddy, lately you've been acting like the cat who swallowed the canary. What's up?"
When I didn't say anything, he pointed the hose at me and said, "Tell me now, or you are one wet cat!"
I just laughed and ran away from the water.

Chapter Seven
A Surprise for the Whole Family

Just as my dad was about to soak me, somebody tapped him on the shoulder. It was my brother Jake.

He said, "Hi, Dad."

My dad dropped the hose and gave Jake a big hug.

He shouted to my mom, "Vanessa, come out here!"

My mom rushed out the door. Then she stopped.

"Jake, you're home!" she said.

Jake said, "Hi, Mom."

Then he winked at me. Our secret was out.

This was his first trip home from college.

And I was the only one he had told about it!

I looked from Dad to Mom. Now Dad had a big goofy grin on his face. And, like I knew she would, Mom was crying.

I had the tissues ready for her.

Jake hugged Mom and I pulled Dad inside.

I needed his help hanging the banner.

When Jake came in, he just stopped and stared.

On the wall, in five different colors, was the banner that
read 'Welcome Home Jake'.

He finally said, "Wow! It's like a welcome rainbow."

Then Dad said, "Ardie made it for you."

Jake smiled and said, "Excellent! Thanks, Little Brother."

When we got back outside, one last thing was in the wagon.
My dad pointed and asked, "Ok, Buddy. What's the ball for?"
"It's for Jamie," I answered. "All he's talked about is how Jake
would come back and teach him soccer. . ."
Before I could finish, Jamie grabbed the ball.
I let him have it. After all, it was his ball.

Soon, Jamie was running around the yard kicking the ball.

Jake was chasing him and the ball.

He stopped to give me a thumbs-up.

Then he said, "You did good, Little Brother."

I smiled because I thought so too.

My mom laughed and said, "Hmmm. Ardie, if I didn't know better, I'd think you liked sharing."

I laughed too and said, "Well, maybe just sometimes!"

CPSIA information can be obtained
at www.ICGtesting.com
Printed in the USA
LVHW072331100419
613761LV00020B/66/P